To my children and
grandchildren.
You are my superheroes.

MY SUPER POWERS: GIFT OF FAITH

Illustrations by Dan McCollam in conjunction with
Pixton Comics, Inc., Pixton.com.

Cover design by Paul Wayland Lee.
PaulWaylandLee.com

Published by Sounds of the Nations.
SoundsoftheNations.com

SOUNDS OF
THE NATIONS

ISBN-13: 978-1493576296
ISBN-10: 1493576291

DEAR PARENT,

My Super Powers is a series of children's books based on the nine gifts of the Holy Spirit mentioned in 1 Corinthians 12:8-9. I believe that children can and should be activated in the gifts of the Spirit at an early age.

To help you facilitate that activation, each *My Super Powers* book contains the following features:

1. A **SUPER POWER STORY** sharing how Timmy and his mother discover various gifts of the Spirit and what that gift could look like in the life of a child.

2. A **BIBLE TIME PAGE** that gives Bible references for further exploration of each gift of the Spirit and for any Bible stories mentioned during the book.

3. A **TALK TIME PAGE** for sparking discussions with your children about the story and their own spiritual gifts.

4. A **PRAYER TIME PAGE** to pray for gifts of the Holy Spirit and then activate them in a simple, practical way.

Gift of
Faith

by Dan McCollam

Timmy and Mom
went on a long trip
to visit his grandma
who was very sick.
Timmy was worried
and tried hard to pray,
but words just weren't
coming to Timmy that day.

The car ride was quiet
as they traveled along
until Mother suggested
they both sing a song.
"I don't feel like singing,"
young Timmy said,
"Too many worries
are stuck in my head."

"What if Grandma
is getting worse?
What if her sickness
doesn't reverse?
What if she doesn't
get better at all?
Mom, stop the car!
Let's give her a call!"

"Wait just a minute,"
Mom said to her son.
"God's in control, and
His will shall be done.
We must have faith
in what God can do.
We know He is good,
and His Word is true!"

"But He doesn't seem
very good today,
with Grandma so sick
and us far away.
It's hard to sing
and even harder to pray.
What can I do when
there are no words to
say?"

"Remember the gifts of the Spirit?" Mom asked. So Timmy thought back to his Sunday School class.

Mom said, "I know exactly the gift that you need. It's the gift of faith that will help you believe."

"That is what I need,"
Timmy said with a choke.
"I try to believe, but my
believer is broke."

Mom said to Timmy,
"I know how you feel..."

"...but that just isn't true
and that thought isn't real.

No matter what kind
of trouble there is,
when we need faith most
God gives us His.
God gives us the power
to trust and to rest.
He helps us to hope
and believe for the best!"

Remember the story
of a troubled young child?
He could not speak, and
his actions were wild.
His father asked Jesus,
"Please help if you can."
So Jesus took time to
answer the man.
"Everything's possible
for the one who believes.
If you will ask,
then you will receive."

"I do believe, but
please help my unbelief!"
cried the desperate father
who was seeking relief.

So Jesus gave
a strong command
and took the young boy
by the hand...

"...the boy stood up
healed and free
and hugged his father
happily!"

So Timmy bowed
his head to pray
and asked for the
gift of faith that day.
Slowly, peace
swept over Tim,
and he knew he
could believe again.

And as the family
drove along
they both joined
in a happy song.
Now they trusted
through and through
and believed for what
their faith could do.

THE
END

BIBLE TIME

The spiritual gift of Gift of Faith is found in **1 Corinthians 12:9**. Everyone has some faith, but the Gift of Faith is God's special power to trust and believe.

Our *My Super Powers* story on Gift of Faith includes an example from the life of Jesus. Jesus encountered a young boy who couldn't speak and was acting very wild because of an evil spirit. The father confessed that he believed in Jesus but then cried out for more faith. God answered his prayer and healed his son, setting him completely free.

Read more in Mark 9:17-27. You can also read the story in Matthew 17:14-20.

TALK TIME

Why was it hard for Timmy to pray for his grandmother?

Have you ever felt like your believer was broke – that is, that it was hard to pray, sing, or believe?

What should you do when it is hard to trust or believe in God or His promises?

Read Luke 17:5-6. What does the Bible say that faith the size of a mustard seed can do?

How big do you think a mustard seed is?

How big do you think the faith is that God has given you?

What can even a little bit of faith do?

PRAYER TIME

Do you have an area of your life in which you need to ask God for His super power of faith?

Do you have a friend or family member who is sick or who has a huge need that it is sometimes hard to believe for? Ask God for a gift of faith to believe in the area of that need.

Remember that God can speak through words, pictures, ideas, feelings, and, of course, the Bible. Did you hear or sense God speaking to you about your need or promise? What did He say? Declare out loud what God has said to you. Declare your faith in what He has said to you and in what He has promised in His Word.

Is there anything you need to act on from what God has said?

OTHER SUPER POWERS STORIES

Word of Wisdom

Word of Knowledge

Gifts of Healing

Working of Miracles

Gift of Prophecy

Discernment of Spirits

Gift of Tongues

Interpretation of Tongues

31636790R00022

Made in the USA
Charleston, SC
24 July 2014